Lily Pig's Book of COLORS

Story and Pictures
by Amye Rosenberg

A GOLDEN BOOK · NEW YORK
Western Publishing Company, Inc., Racine, Wisconsin 53404

ISBN 0-307-02155-6   MCMXCII

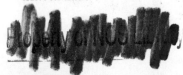

Today was Lily Pig's birthday, and what a glorious sunny day it was!

"I want to have a picnic in the backyard," thought Lily Pig. "I'll invite my friends, and we'll celebrate this day together."

So, dressed in her best red jacket, Lily Pig went to
buy things for her birthday picnic. She swung her basket
and skipped along the road to town.

"A good party needs balloons," Lily Pig thought. So, first thing, she bought a bunch of bright red balloons. She admired them as she walked along.

But all of a sudden, the Hedgehog children swung out of a tree where they were playing.

"Surprise!" they giggled. They crashed into the red balloons with their prickly spines.

Pop! Pop! **Red** pops everywhere!

"Oh, dear," thought Lily Pig. "Now that my red balloons are gone, I'll need party favors for my friends."

She went into a shop that was full of goodies. "Those blue pencils would be nice," she said, pointing to a high shelf.

"Just jump up and help yourself," said the rabbit clerk.

Lily Pig did just that. But since pigs cannot jump as well as rabbits—

It rained **blue** pencils on Lily Pig!

Lily Pig headed for the market square to see what goodies she could find there. Outside a shop, she saw a cage of yellow baby chicks. They were so sweet and fluffy that she wanted to pet them. So Lily Pig unlatched the cage door, and—

She got lots of tickles from lots of **yellow** chicks!

When the chicks were safely back in their cage, Lily
Pig walked on into the square. There she saw a dog who
was selling grapes, plums, and umbrellas.

"I need an umbrella, in case it rains on my birthday
picnic," thought Lily Pig.

She tried a big purple one to see how it worked. The
umbrella popped open so quickly that Lily Pig fell
backward into the grapes and plums, and—

Everything went **purple**!

Lily Pig decided that the supermarket would be the best place to find yummy things to eat.

She loved riding on the back of the shopping cart. As she whizzed down a long aisle she thought about making orange juice for her picnic. Then—*crash!*

Oranges everywhere—and **orange** juice!

Lily Pig hurriedly left the supermarket. Outside, she saw Ma Gator selling crunchy green pickles.

"I can't have a picnic without pickles!" thought Lily Pig. She dipped into the barrel for them. She dipped deeper and deeper, until—*splash!*

A great **green** pickley splash!

Lily Pig trotted away, wringing the pickle juice from her jacket. She did not see Mr. Crow working in the road, and she tripped over his bucket—*plop!*

She fell into a puddle of gooey **black** tar.

"Oh, dear!" thought Lily Pig. "I must clean up, or I'll never have a picnic today. I haven't even invited my friends yet!" She rushed home.

She filled her white bathtub with white soapy
bubbles. She took a big **white** bar of soap and scrubbed
off the tar and pickle juice and sticky fruit goo.

Soon Lily Pig was a clean **pink** pig again. She was drying herself with a soft pink towel when she heard a commotion outside.

She rushed straight out into the yard to see what it could be.

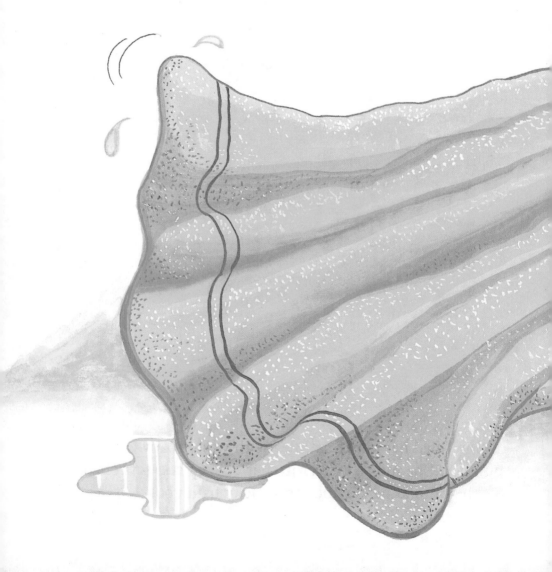

"Surprise! Happy birthday to you!" sang Lily Pig's friends. They had brought armloads of gifts and balloons.

Lily Pig blushed behind her pink towel. She certainly was surprised!

So Lily Pig celebrated her birthday with a backyard picnic after all. And the best part was a huge **brown** chocolate cake with lots of candles on it.

Each candle was a different color. How many colors can you find?